To Maile —
Always do your best in life
    and love will do the rest!
♡ Judy Walker 2014

Turkey Trouble

by Judy Walker

WestBow Press books may be ordered through booksellers or by contacting:

WestBow Press
A Division of Thomas Nelson & Zondervan
1663 Liberty Drive
Bloomington, IN 47403
www.westbowpress.com
1 (866) 928-1240

ISBN: 978-1-4908-3233-3 (sc)
ISBN: 978-1-4908-4371-1 (hc)
ISBN: 978-1-4908-3234-0 (e)
Library of Congress Control Number: 2014905906

Printed in the United States by Bookmasters
Ashland, OH
July 2014
50005541

WESTBOW®
PRESS
A DIVISION OF THOMAS NELSON
& ZONDERVAN

To my precious grandchildren
Matthew, Grace, Faith, and Caleb
Always do your best in life and love will do the rest!
God loves you so much and so do I!

Acknowledgements

This story began 38 years ago in a first grade classroom in Council Bluffs, Iowa, with two little puppets named Pokey and Tillie. My teaching partner, Jeanette Ryan, and I entertained and instructed our students using puppetry. The children related enthusiastically to the characters and the challenges they faced daily in 1975. Even today, children face the same challenges, and so the story evolved and grew in my mind over the years to become TURKEY TROUBLE. A big thank you goes to Jeanette for being my teaching partner and the creativity she brought to the characters of Pokey and Tillie. You were a huge inspiration to me in developing and bringing resolution to the story which began in our classroom so many years ago.

A giant shout-out goes to Kathy Kerber, the illustrator of TURKEY TROUBLE. The characters and the story have lived in my mind for many years and Kathy brought those images to life on the pages of TURKEY TROUBLE. Thank you for helping me tell the story in pictures, as well as in words. They are terrific.

To my husband Randy, thank you for your encouragement and belief in the value of this story. You inspired me to write TURKEY TROUBLE and get it printed in a book for children to enjoy! I love you and I am grateful for your confidence in me.

Around golden sun rose in the sky over Yummy-Yummy Land on this very special day. Today was the day the King would inspect the turkeys at his Royal Turkey Ranch.

The King's vision of the fat, juicy birds with rainbow-colored feathers made his mouth water and his eyes glisten with delight as he dressed in his royal robes and got ready to depart for the ranch.

"Bring my royal carriage to the front of the palace, Coachman!" the King ordered excitedly. As he climbed into the carriage, Wise Sir Who perched on his shoulder and they made their short journey to the ranch.

When they arrived, the King commanded, "Line up, my turkeys, and march past me, two by two. I want to see you in all your beauty and splendor!"

What a procession it was! Turkeys were here and there and everywhere… everywhere but in a line two by two. The King could not believe his eyes. Never had he seen or heard such ornery, ill-mannered turkeys.

"This will never do!" cried the King. He shook his head in despair. "These birds are a disgrace to Yummy-Yummy Land! These turkeys are tough."

It was a very discouraged King who returned to the palace that night. "Whatever shall we do? Tough turkeys are terrible!" These words echoed through the royal bedroom all night long.

At breakfast the King could not eat a bite. He was crying into his bowl of royal oatmeal when Wise Sir Who flew into the dining room. He landed on the King's shoulder and thoughtfully hooted, "Hire a helper, Your Highness."

A smile lit up the King's sad face. "Yes, a helper to train my turkeys! That is exactly what I need! Today I will choose a trainer who will make those tough turkeys into the tender, fine feathered birds they should be."

"Messengers," he summoned, "send the royal call to every corner of the kingdom today that the King will hire the best turkey trainer in the land."

The applicants came from far and near. "Bring them in and let them convince me who is the best."

The first did a fancy little tap dance and then bowed at the feet of the King. "I, my King, am Tippy-Toes TuTu, the Turkey Trotter. I will teach the turkeys to twist and tap without tripping and tangling their toes in their tails."

"Hmmm...a fine idea," thought the King. "Next!" he called.

"I am Timothy Tuxedo, the Turkey Tailor, Your Majesty," declared the second proudly. "If I am chosen, I will tastefully dress the turkeys in trousers and tights."

"Royal turkeys certainly do need good dressing," reflected the King. "But bring on the next one. I must see them all before I choose my turkey trainer."

The third one was a traveling troubadour who strummed his guitar and sang a beautiful melody with these words. "I'm Tennessee Tyler, the Turkey Tenor, and I'll teach the turkeys to twitter tunefully."

"Lovely," praised the King. "Those turkeys' voices could certainly use some improvement!"

As he said these words, his eyes fell on a dark corner of the room and he saw a tiny turkey in the shadows who looked at him timidly, with trustful eyes.

"I am Tillie," she said in a tiny voice.

"You are sweet and beautiful," the King admired. "Why aren't you tough like the other turkeys?"

Tillie explained proudly, "I have a friend who is kind and treats me tenderly. I think he would be the perfect turkey trainer for the ranch."

"WHO?" questioned the wise old owl sitting on the King's shoulder.

Tillie spoke up again. "Pokey is his name and he is as good as he is kind. He will treat the turkeys tenderly."

"We all become the way we are treated!" stated Wise Sir Who.

"So that is why you are so sweet and tender! Pokey come forward and bow to the throne," ordered the King.

The gentle little donkey bowed low and said, "At your service, Your Majesty."

"That is exactly what you will be, Pokey—at my service! I can tell from looking at Tillie that you are the best turkey trainer in all the land. You have the job of training my turkeys to become tender!"

"HURRAY!" The King danced with glee. Now he would have terrific turkeys at his Royal Turkey Ranch.

The next day a bright golden sun rose in the sky over Yummy-Yummy Land. Boot Camp for Turkeys would start today.

"Oh my, oh my, Pokey, how can we make these tough turkeys tender?" fussed Tillie.

"Step Number 1, my sweet Tillie! Tender Turkeys must look their BEST!"

As they walked through the gates of the Royal Turkey Ranch, they were greeted by a mob of scraggly creatures whose tail feathers were dustier than the royal maid's feather duster. Breakfast porridge was running down into their wattles. They were scratching, itching, and grumbling as feathers flew everywhere.

"Okey dokey!" shouted Pokey. "You turkeys are about to become tender. You must be clean and look your best! It's shower time."

Tillie helped Pokey line the turkeys up. There was a hurricane of water and suds as the tough turkeys scrubbed the dust off their scraggly feathers.

"Okey dokey!" said Pokey. "Now, Timothy Tuxedo, it is time to dress these turkeys."

"I will tastefully dress the turkeys in trousers and tights," agreed Timothy, the Turkey Tailor. "Line up Turkeys! I will make you look like the fine feathered birds you were meant to be!"

When Timothy had finished dressing them, the turkeys proudly strutted their clean, brightly colored feather fans past Pokey and Tillie.

"These turkeys are beautiful!" admired Tillie.

"Okey dokey! Job number one complete! These turkeys LOOK THEIR BEST!" said Pokey with satisfaction, while Tillie looked on with pride.

Early the next morning the flock of handsome turkeys reported for Day 2 of Boot Camp.

"Okey dokey, Turkeys," shouted Pokey, "training time today means Tender Turkeys must DO THEIR BEST. Turkey Trainers Tippy-Toes TuTu and Tennessee Tyler will train you to be Talented Turkeys."

"Today you fine looking turkeys will learn to twist and tap without tripping and tangling your toes in your tails! Let the lessons begin!" instructed Tippy-Toes TuTu.

The turkeys twisted and turned and tapped in time to the tunes.

"One two three, One two three, One two three," counted TuTu as she taught the turkeys how to Turkey Trot!

Pokey and Tillie tapped their toes as they watched the turkeys twirl to the tunes. "Oh my, oh my!" exclaimed Tillie, flapping her wings in delight. "You made these turkeys terrific dancers, TuTu."

"**O**key dokey!" said Pokey. "Now Turkeys, Tennessee Tyler will teach you a beautiful song to sing. Take it, Tyler!"

Tennessee Tyler strummed his guitar and twittered tunefully.

Love, you Tender Turkeys!
LOOK your BEST!
DO your BEST!
And BE your BEST!
Let Love do all the rest!
Then you'll be Tender, Turkeys!

Pokey and Tillie sighed with joy. The tough turkeys were becoming tender!

"Okey dokey," said Pokey, "tomorrow will be the most important day of training. Tillie, you will be their teacher."

"Oh my, oh my! What can I teach them? They are clean and beautiful and they can sing and dance much better than I can."

"Tillie, they have to learn to be kind to each other. That is the only way they can BE THEIR BEST."

As she went to bed that night, Tillie fretted and worried about how she could get the turkeys to BE THEIR BEST! She knew it would not be easy but she must try her best for Pokey and the King.

She said her prayers and closed her eyes. She tossed and turned and finally fell asleep. Suddenly Pokey heard her cry out in the night.

"Oh my, oh my, Pokey! I can't do it! The turkeys are still tough. How am I ever going to make them tender?" cried Tillie from her sleep.

Pokey jumped from his bed and shook Tillie awake. "Okey dokey, Tillie, wake up! You're having a bad dream."

There were tears running down her face as she told Pokey how the turkeys in her dream were mean to each other.

When morning came, Pokey explained to Tillie how she would train the turkeys to BE THEIR BEST. " Today we will show the turkeys how to be tender. They will learn the Golden Rule. They will learn to treat each other with kindness."

As Pokey and Tillie entered the training field on the third day of boot camp, they heard angry shouts.

"DID NOT!"

"DID TOO!"

"DID NOT!"

"DID TOO!"

The shouts were being led by Tattletale Tessa Turkey on one side and Terrible Terrence on the other side.

"Oh my, oh my!" cried Tillie as she rushed over to the two. "What is the problem?"

Tattletale Tessa shouted, "Terrence pulled my feathers. It hurt!"

"Terrence, tell the truth. Did you pull Tessa's feathers?" questioned Tillie.

"DID NOT!"

"DID TOO!"

"The truth, Terrence!" Tillie insisted.

Terrence hung his head and admitted, "Well, maybe I did just a little."

"See, I told you he did!" Tessa bragged.

Pokey was whispering in Terrence's ear as Tillie tried to smooth Tessa's ruffled feathers.

"Terrence, you must always tell the truth!"

Terrence trotted slowly toward Tessa and timidly managed to say, "I'm sorry," the magic words that would make everything better.

Tessa and Terrence hugged and Tillie and Pokey breathed a sigh of relief as the other turkeys cheered.

"That wasn't as hard as I thought it would be," said Tillie, glowing with pride. "Now these turkeys are tender."

"Not so fast, Tillie," said Pokey.

"Oh my, oh my!" fretted Tillie. "What now?"

From the other side of the training yard a group of tough turkeys were laughing and shouting.

"Oh my, oh my," said Tillie, as she and Pokey pushed through the crowd to see what was going on. Little Tina Turkey, sobbing loudly, was lying in a mud puddle and covered with mud.

"Tina, what happened?" Tillie questioned as she helped Tina up.

"I tripped on someone's foot and landed in the mud. I look terrible."

"Oh my, oh my! Let me help!" soothed Tillie, as she wiped the mud from Tina's beak and the tears from her eyes. She hugged Tina. "There, there," she comforted. "You look beautiful again!"

"Okey dokey!" said Pokey sternly to the tough turkeys who had been laughing at Tina. "Tillie is right. Laughing at someone who is hurt is what tough turkeys do. Tender turkeys show love and tenderness. They help others."

The turkeys who had been laughing at Tina hung their heads.

"I tripped Tina," confessed Tommy. "I'm sorry, Tina."

"Laughing at someone is mean," said one turkey from the crowd.

"We were tough turkeys to Tina."

"Yes, we want to be tender like Tillie," shouted another turkey.

"Okey dokey," said Pokey. "All you have to do is treat others like you want to be treated, with love and tenderness. That's what friends are for. Everyone needs friends who show love!"

"Hurray!" shouted the turkeys. "We promise to be Tender!"

Pokey and Tillie high fived each other and sang:

Love, you Tender Turkeys!
LOOK your BEST!
DO your BEST!
And BE your BEST!
Let Love do all the rest!
Then you'll be Tender, Turkeys!

"We did it!" the turkeys all shouted. Tillie and Pokey had proved themselves to be terrific turkey trainers. The King would be proud of these tender turkeys.

At last the day had come for the King of Yummy-Yummy Land to pick the tenderest birds at the Royal Turkey Ranch for his Royal Feast.

Wise Sir Who was perched on his shoulder as he ate his royal oatmeal for breakfast.

"I had a dream last night," the King told Sir Who. "In the dream, there were rows and rows of tender turkeys and it was hard for me to choose the best. What do you think my dream means?"

"WHO you choose will be difficult, Your Highness," predicted the Wise Owl. "If your dream comes true, Tillie and Pokey will have done a terrific job of training those terrible turkeys."

After breakfast the King summoned his royal carriage to take him to the ranch.

"We will soon see if Pokey and Tillie were able to train the terrible turkeys," said the King anxiously as they got closer. When the royal carriage entered the gate of the ranch, the King's eyes sparkled with delight and amazement. The turkeys were everything he had dreamed they would be. They were clean and well behaved, and even more terrific than he had imagined.

"Sir Who, choosing the best turkeys for my feast will be very difficult. They all look perfect."

Pokey and Tillie bowed and greeted the King as he stepped from the royal carriage with Sir Who on his shoulder.

"My Royal Turkey Trainers," said the King, "the turkeys are splendid. How did you make them so tender?"

"Okey dokey," said Pokey. "I will tell you the three simple secrets to the success of these turkeys: Tender Turkeys LOOK THEIR BEST, DO THEIR BEST, and BE THEIR BEST."

"Ingenious!" praised Wise Sir Who.

But the King looked upset. He was thinking to himself, "How will I ever pick the best turkeys for my feast with all of them so perfect?"

He walked up and down the rows of perfectly trained turkeys. He asked each one, "How did you become so tender?"

Shy little Tina Turkey had the answer. "We had our teacher, Tillie, who loved us."

Tommy, Tessa, and Terrence agreed. "We learned to love each other like we love ourselves. Tillie taught us about love." The other turkeys agreed. All you need is love.

The King left the Royal Turkey Ranch with a very difficult decision to make. "Who shall I pick for my Royal Feast? I want the best, the most tender turkeys. Who shall they be, Sir Who?"

"I cannot say WHO, for the decision is Your Majesty's."

That night the King had another dream and he awoke the next morning with a smile on his face.

He ordered his Royal Secretary to write his choice on the Royal Stationery. "Deliver this Royal Decree by noon today!" he commanded.

Who had been chosen for the King's feast? No one but the King knew the answer.

At noon all of the turkeys gathered around Pokey as he broke open the King's seal and proceeded to read the declaration.

I hereby declare
Tillie, the Most Tender Turkey
She and her friends Tessa, Tina, Tommy, and Terrence
Will be escorted to the palace in one week
To be dressed and prepared for the Royal Feast
Your Royal Majesty, the King

I, your Majesty the King hereby declare Tillie the most tender turkey in all of Yummy Yummy Land

Tillie and her friends clapped their hands in delight. They had been chosen by the King! They were filled with joy!

"Pokey, I can't believe it! The King chose me!! I am going to be a guest at the King's feast! I'm so lucky!" exclaimed Tillie as she jumped up and down and hugged her friend who had helped her be her tender best.

Pokey had tears running down his cheeks, but they weren't tears of joy.

"Pokey, why are you crying when I am so happy?"

"Tillie, I fear you are not a guest for dinner."

"Oh my, oh my, what else could I be?"

"Dinner, I fear, my dear Tillie."

"What? The King is going to eat me?" shrieked Tillie. "Oh my, oh my! Whatever shall we do?" Tears of fear rolled down her face and she was full of despair.

Pokey wiped his tears and he looked determined.

"Okey dokey, Tillie. Let's not panic. We must get a plan to save you and the others. I will think of something."

"Oh my, oh my, we only have a week, Pokey! PLEASE THINK FAST!"

Pokey sat down to think, with his head cradled in his hooves. As he chewed on a piece of hay, an idea came to him!

"I've got it!" he exclaimed. "Okey dokey, Tillie, you and the other turkeys are officially on a diet! The King will not want skinny turkeys for his feast. This week you will eat nothing but disgusting worms and bugs."

"Oh my, oh my! I don't like to be hungry, and I really don't like worms and bugs for dinner," complained Tillie.

"Tillie, my dear, you have only two choices: SKIP DINNER or BE DINNER for the King."

"Oh my, oh my, to save my life, I will start my diet today."

The turkeys all chanted, "Save Tillie, Save Tillie!"

To save her life and the lives of her friends, the work began. They ran, did sit-ups, push-ups, bench presses, and jumped rope from early morning until late at night. Dinner was a tiny bowl of worms topped with a few juicy bugs. Before bed each night the turkeys were weighed and measured. Each day they did the same things again.

After three days Terrence, Tommy, Tessa, and Tina were looking very skinny--not at all like the plump birds that the King had chosen for his feast.

BUT NOT TILLIE! She seemed to be fatter than before, and the curious thing was, no one could tell why. The other turkeys cheered her on with their chant of "Save Tillie! Save Tillie!" while she worked out.

Tillie seemed nervous and fidgety and Pokey was worried. If his plan for her to lose weight didn't succeed, Tillie was in trouble and she was running out of time. The feast was in two days.

"Okey dokey, Tillie, we have a problem. Tell Pokey what is going on. Why are you gaining weight?" Pokey reached down to get a piece of straw to chew on like he always did when he was thinking. Suddenly his paw hit on something in the straw--a stash of chocolate bars.

Tillie hung her head, ashamed that she had been caught cheating on her diet. Tears filled her eyes and she confessed that her nerves had gotten the best of her. She had broken the rules and now she would have to pay for it. There was no way she could escape being the King's special turkey for his feast.

Pokey looked sadly at his friend. Tomorrow her fate would be sealed when the royal carriage came to take the chosen turkeys to the palace.

The carriage arrived early the next morning, and it was a sad goodbye as the turkeys staying behind at the ranch waved a tearful farewell to their friends. Would they ever see them again? They wondered. Pokey stood alone in the shadows and shed huge tears of grief. He was heartbroken to lose his treasured friends.

Just as the carriage was about to pull away from the ranch, the driver shouted, "Pokey, by order of the King, you are to help pull the carriage to the palace and be a guest at the feast."

Obediently, Pokey replied, "Okey dokey."

He heard Tillie say, "Oh my, oh my! At least you will be with me, Pokey, when I fulfill the order of the King."

When the royal carriage arrived at the palace, they were met by the King who had a huge smile on his face!

"Welcome, my fine turkeys! Come inside and get ready for the feast. Tessa, Tina, Tommy, and Terrence, follow Sir Who to the Royal Dressing Room. As for you, Tillie, I have special plans for you."

"Oh my, oh my, my King! I can assure you, I am nothing special," insisted Tillie.

"But you are!" assured the King. "That is why you were chosen as the Best Turkey for the Feast. Let us go to the kitchen and see what my royal chefs have already prepared!"

Tillie obediently followed the King to the Royal Kitchen, shaking and quivering every step of the way.

The chefs all stood at attention as the King and Tillie entered the kitchen. The aroma of delicious food was incredible! Tillie's mouth began to water, and then she remembered that the King had chosen her to be a part of this meal.

Tillie bravely stood before the King and looked him in the eye. "My King, it is an honor to be chosen by you for this Royal Feast. I am ready to be prepared by the cooks for you to enjoy."

The King glowed with pride and satisfaction. He knew he had chosen the best turkey! "I will see you at the Feast!" said the King as he left the Royal Kitchen. "My chefs will take good care of you, my sweet Tillie!"

The head chef said to Tillie, "Follow me."

She was led into a room filled with velvet and linen cloths.

"Oh my, oh my! How strange! This is not the way you prepare a turkey for dinner," protested Tillie.

"Yes, it is! This is how we prepare the turkey who is THE BEST! You are to be dressed in a royal purple robe because you are the guest of honor! You were chosen by the King to sit with him and enjoy the Royal Feast! Now put on your robe and go to the Royal Dining Room! The King is waiting for you!"

Tears streamed down Tillie's face. "Oh my, oh my!" sobbed the beautiful turkey. "The King chose me. I am not dinner, but a guest for dinner!" Her mouth began to water as she thought of the delicious food she would get to enjoy.

As Tillie entered the Royal Dining Room, a trumpet signaled for everyone to stand. They all clapped and cheered for the little turkey who had helped her friend, Pokey, train the turkeys at the Royal Turkey Ranch.

Tillie took her seat next to the King and the program began.

"Introducing the Four T's," announced the Herald.

Out twirled Tina and Tessa dressed in tutus, followed by Tommy and Terence in tuxedos. The girls tapped and twisted to the tune as the boys twittered, "Love, You Tender Turkeys."

Everyone clapped and cheered when the song was over!

Bowing before the King and Tillie, Terence said, "We all love you, Tillie, for teaching us how to be our best! You truly are the best!"

There were hugs all around, and the King had tears in his eyes as he watched all the love.

But the evening wasn't over yet! Wise Sir Who, sitting on the King's shoulder, cleared his throat. "WHO is missing at this feast?" he asked Tillie.

"My best friend, Pokey!"

Just then the doors to the Royal Banquet Room opened and in came Pokey. He approached the throne, bowed to the King, and then gave Tillie a wink.

"Your Highness and Sir Who, you made a wise choice when you chose Tillie. She is good and kind and always shows love. Love is all you need to be tender!"

With tears in her eyes and love in her heart, Tillie looked at her faithful friend. "Pokey, I love you. You were the one that helped me become the BEST I could be."

Wise Sir Who said, "That's what friends are for!"

"Let the Feast begin!" ordered the King.

Everyone at the feast had a wonderful time, and the King promised to have a feast every year to celebrate his Tender Turkeys!

That night as the sun went down in Yummy -Yummy Land, tummies were full of food and hearts were full of love. It had been the best day and many more would come for the turkeys at the Royal Turkey Ranch. They had learned from Pokey and Tillie a lesson they would never forget:

LOVE MAKES TURKEYS TENDER AND
TENDER TURKEYS ARE BEST!